Planet Pregnancy

Planet Pregnancy

Linda Oatman High

FRONT STREET
Honesdale, Pennsylvania

Library of Congress Cataloging-in-Publication Data

High, Linda Oatman.
Planet Pregnancy / Linda Oatman High.—1st ed.
p. cm.
Summary: Sixteen-year-old Sahara struggles with an unplanned pregnancy,
and all its conflicting emotions, in this novel told in free verse.
ISBN 978-1-59078-584-3 (hardcover : alk. paper)
[1. Novels in verse. 2. Pregnancy—Fiction. 3. Teenage mothers—Fiction.] I. Title.

PZ7.5.H54Pl 2008
[Fic]—dc22
2007049586
Paperback ISBN 978-1-59078-767-0

FRONT STREET
An Imprint of Boyds Mills Press, Inc.
815 Church Street
Honesdale, Pennsylvania 18431

Trimester One

Nice Girls Keep Their Legs Together

It's September tenth and
I'm holding my breath
because life
and death
and everything
in-between
depends
on a stick
dipped
for less than
ten seconds
in a dish
of pee.

Ten, nine, eight …
I can't freaking wait …
Seven, six, five …
To know if there's
something alive …
Four, three, two …
Or will the line be blue?
One …
Done.
This is so
not fun.
I lift the stick
from the dish.
I wish
that this

was somebody
else's ten seconds
tonight.
Not mine.

It bites,
when everything
depends
on one stupid
blue line.

Half-praying,
waiting
the three minutes
it says in the directions,
I whisper a confession
to Jesus and Mary
and the saints,
feeling as if
I could faint.
I hate
suspense.
Tense, sweating,
almost wetting
my pants,
I can't
stand to look
at the stick.

I lick
my lips,
sip Pepsi,
breathe in,
breathe out.
Keep my
heart beating.

The three minutes
are finished, I think.
I peek,
and the line
on the stick
is pink.
I dump
the pee
in the sink.

I'm only sixteen.
I'm not a geek.
I was the Dixie Queen
at school last week.
I shimmered, glimmered
with sequins
and a tiara.

My name's Sahara,
like the desert.

Unlike the Badlands,
though,
I'm not barren.

Dustin doesn't know.
Not yet.

His cousin wasn't
even pregnant
one month, and
she went in a panic
to the clinic
for a "termination."
(It sounds more humane
than saying "operation"
or "abortion" or "getting
rid of It.")

I'm in deep shit.
Deep shit's in me.

My body is not
the Badlands.

Texas is
the runner-up state
for teenage
pregnancies,

says the newspaper.
California is
Number One.
It must be
all that sun.

When I'm out
of school,
I think it'd be cool
to drive
to Hollywood
or Dollywood.
(Anywhere but
Wally World.)

I'm saving
my waitressing
paychecks
for a Lexus.

But sex
is big
in Texas.

What if
I never
get my Lexus?

Maybe a baby
will be my
runner-up dream:
the next
best thing
for me.

I'm so
totally alone
in what I
know
about the hidden
forbidden
insides of
me, and
all because
of EPT.

It's not easy
to be the
one and only
lonely resident
of Planet Pregnancy.

I wish I'd listened
to my big sister's
advice.

"Nice girls
keep their legs
together," Heather whispered.
"Never wear
low-cut
thong-butt
leather,
and feathers, and red
all together.
It makes you seem
easy. Cheap. Sleazy."

"Who cares
how I *seem*
to be? I'm
just me!"

I never
thought I'd be
living (barely)
on the scary
Planet Pregnancy:
still just me
but changed
forever, while
Heather
remains
the same.

It's September eleventh,
and everybody's remembering
how thousands
went to heaven
together,
just flew
into the blue
on that terrible
unbearable
morning.

There's a terror
warning
today, and I
try to pray.
Thoughts get
in my brain's way,
and I'm ashamed,
because I
remember thinking
on that September
day:
I'm glad it wasn't me.
I'm glad
that bad
and sad
tragedy happens
to other people,

not me.
It's always
somebody else.

Until now.

Wow.
Now *I'm* the
catastrophe.
I turn off the TV,
because *I'm* enough
bad news for me.

I'm spending
my paycheck
on a psychic:
Madam Mystic,
the Extrasensory
Telekinetic
Expert.
She works
from a dirty room
in a purple mobile home.
She uses a snow globe
as a crystal ball,
and an almost-bald
parrot calls,

"Hey you! Hello!"
Candles flicker,
and incense smoke
floats into my nose.

"What's the sex
of the Embryo?"
That's what
I want to know.
(I call it
the Embryo
or the Egg
because it gags me
to imagine a
human being
floating
like Coast soap
in the
Sea of Me.)

Madam Mystic
has a lisp
and a wisp
of mustache
above her lip.

"I thee
a penith,"
she whispers.

"It ith
a boy
and will
arrive on
wingth of joy."

I know
this sounds
rude,
but I've
had way
enough
of dudes.
Male
genitalia
should be
locked up
in jail
so it's
not knocking
up
any more
poor
girls like I
now seem to be:
defenseless,
senseless.

Penises should
be illegal.

Or at least
kept
on a leash,
like a
freaking
beast.

After the psychic,
I hike to the clinic.
(I'm walking so that
nobody notices
my car
parked outside
of strange places.
Here in the boondocks
people like to gossip
about anything possible.)

This clinic
is where Dustin's cousin
had It Taken Care Of.
It's in a scary part
of town. I look around,
paranoid.
The word *clinic,*

painted in faded brown,
is missing the letter *l.*

The waiting room
is crowded
with girls, heads bowed,
slouching down,
as if they wish
to disappear.
I bet they're like me:
not believing
that they are Really
Here or that this is
Really Real.

One girl
jiggles a flip-flop
and picks at the skin
on her heel.
Another one
looks like a cheerleader.
She's weeping,
not caring who hears,
and it seems like
she just can't deal.
I know just
how she feels.

The plastic chairs
are fluorescent orange:
the blinding bright color
of a danger sign
on a construction site.
I go up to the desk,
and the receptionist
isn't very receptive.

"It's necessary
to have an
appointment,"
she hisses.

Melissa,
reads her name tag.

She talks
through her nose,
like siphoning
gas through a hose.
There's a rose
on her desk,
and I wonder
who would give
her something like that.
She probably
gave it to
herself.

"I didn't make
a date," I say.
"But it's an urgency.
An emergency. I just
need ten seconds."

"Ten
seconds
can't change
anything, you know."

Melissa
is a psycho.
Cynical and spastic,
way too sarcastic,
she's wearing elastic-waist
pants.
She's a bitch, the
Wicked Witch of
West Texas.

"Forget it.
Let it go.
I'll just
go home
if nobody wants
to help me."

"Have a
nice afternoon,"
Melissa
croons.

"Oh, way.
You do too."
I can be
sarcastic,
too.

This is
the pits.
I have
zits.

I'm craving
like crazy:
Kit-Kats
and Bits-O-Honey
and Sunny Delight.
Breyer's Light
and dark hot chocolate,
hot dogs and cheese logs
and Brie cheese
and linguini with butter.
Slim Jims
and Popsicles

and dill pickles
and chips with
dip.

I wish
I could zip
my lips shut.
My butt
is a bubble,
a sign
of the trouble
ahead for me.

I can't stop eating,
feeding my face
in a race
to nowhere.
"She must
be in a growth
spurt," Mom says
to my brother Curt.

"Look at her butt
and her gut!
She's a chub.
Sahara's joining
the Fat Girls
Club."

My brother
is
such
a
dweeb.

"I'm too
fatigued
to speak
to such
a geek,"
I say.
Then I lay
on my bed,
beneath a poster
of Johnny Depp,
where I sleep
and dream
of being
the old me.

"You're such a grouch.
You're like always
on the couch," Heather says.
"All you do is watch TV.
How freakin' lazy
can an
almost-seventeen-

year-old girl
be?"

Heather's guess
is that I have PMS,
and that's why
I'm such a mess.

I'm tired.
I was fired
from the diner.
The boss at
Sauce and Toss
said that
it was because
I'm whiny.
And slow.
But he doesn't know
what's inside
of me.

Neither does
my family.

If they
only knew,
they'd understand
why I'm a member

of the Church of
the Couch
and the TV.

Ms. Ledman,
the phys ed teacher,
keeps yelling at me
to run faster
or I won't pass
gym class.
Obviously,
I'm flunking
the eight-minute
mile test.
I'm doing my
pregnant best.
This macadam track
is like the highway
to hell.
I don't feel well.

Ms. Ledman has no idea
how tired
I am.
Other kids
in gym
have no idea
why I'm so quiet

or why I try to hide
behind the locker
while changing
into gym clothes.
They wonder why
Miss Social Butterfly
has crept
into a cocoon.
Soon enough,
they'll know.
I can't try to hide it
forever.

Even my best friend Emma
doesn't know.
I'm on an island:
sometimes
trying to survive,
at other times
resigned to not being
alive.
I don't even want
to drive,
which usually
makes me feel so alive,
and I *so* don't
want to exercise.
The Dixie Queen
will never be seen

again.
She's dead.

I forgot
my deodorant today,
and no way
do I want to sweat.
Ms. Ledman
should just let
me sit on the bench.
I wish I'd forged
a gym excuse.
I have no idea
why the eight-minute mile
is so freaking
important, anyway.
I hate to run.
It is so not fun.

The September sun
feels like July.
(I wish that *I* could just
go back in time, to July,
and then
I wouldn't be
pregnant.)
It's such a bummer:
Running.
How will this help me in

the Real World?
When will I need running
in Real Life?
Will my future require
running?
Maybe.
If there's a baby.
I'll have to chase it.
I hate to run.
It's so
not fun.

On Halloween Eve
I'm eating
three Lean Cuisines,
for trick or treat.

I'm even eating
the green beans.

I'm still wearing
my jeans,
which hang low
below the Embryo.
The Embryo
doesn't know
that it's making
me fat

or that
it's making
me crave
food
that I usually
hate.
It doesn't know
that it's making
me grow
huge boobs.

It doesn't mean
to be rude, I know,
but this Egg
that grows, curled,
inside of me
is taking over
my world.

It tells me
when to eat
or sleep.
I weep
even over
lame game
shows on TV.

"Trick or treat!"
scream
the costumed kids
who keep
showing up with
pumpkin buckets
crammed
too full
of candy.
I hand out treats
wearing my old
clown suit,
which is no longer
so cute.

Curt's in cowboy boots
and a ten-gallon hat,
and Heather
has a cardboard bat
taped on her chest.
A little girl in the best
Cinderella dress
shows up with a pest
of a Ninja brother,
and I think,
He could be mine,
in a few years.
I feel the tears
start to come.

I'm bummed.
Halloween
used to be
fun.

I hand the candy
to Heather.
"I'm going to bed.
My head
is exploding.
There's so much pain,
like a migraine.
It's killing me."
What's really killing me,
though,
is something
so scary:
something
that nobody
knows.

Curt is obsessed
with Xbox LIVE.
I think that the headset
has grown
into his head.

My brother fires
a pretend gun
in some
violent video
game, chatting
into thin air
with people
that he can't
see.

"They're from all over the globe!
It's socialization!"
That's Curt's rationalization
for wasting
so many days
staring at the TV
screen.

If Curt only knew
that I now exist
on my very own
planet,
maybe he'd come to visit
his sister
instead of being obsessed
with people
that he doesn't
even
know.

I miss
my Big
Bro.

I'm in the Gloom Room:
the despised guidance
office at school,
because I need
guidance.
I'm thinking of confiding:
telling Mr. Felter
about my predicament.
I chicken out, though,
because I just know
that he'll call my mother.

There's no
free guidance
in this situation.
No easy answers.
It's like cancer:
something growing
without my permission.

Mr. Felter's hair
is all helter-skelter,
and he looks like
a hospital patient
or a crazy professor.

"What's the matter, Sahara?"
he asks.
"Boyfriend troubles?
Parent problems?
Poor grades?
Depression?"

This session
is obviously
not the answer
to the question
that I'm carrying
inside.
I'm not ready
to confide
or confess.

"I guess it's nothing," I say.
"Well, maybe just that
I'm having some trouble
in Mrs. Futer's class.
I need a tutor,
fast."
Mr. Felter
hitches
up his belt,
like he's a cowboy,
happy to be
important.

"Report to the office
tomorrow," he says.
"One tutor,
coming right up.
That'll brighten
your life."

What I really need,
I wish I could confide,
is one less life
inside.

Trimester Two

The Great Date Rape

It's Thanksgiving,
and next week
I'll be just another
girl living, existing,
in this world
for seventeen
years.

It's early morning,
and the thirty-pound bird
is in the sink.
It weighs more
than four normal
newborn babies.

"Who's going to eat
all that meat?"
I ask. "It looks sick.
Quick! Get it out of
the sink.
I think
I'm going to puke.
I must have caught
that stupid flu
that's going around
in school."

Mom's yanking
that packet
of turkey neck
and gizzard
from the hidden
insides
of the raw,
thawed bird.

"Happy Thanksgiving!"
she says,
too perky.

"That poor turkey,"
I say,
and I go lay
on the sofa.
I try to doze,
but soon enough
the smells
of turkey
and stuffing
turn my stomach.
I usually love this:
the smells
of Thanksgiving.

"Oh, no.
I think I'm going to
throw up.
Mom!"

I heave,
making believe
that it's
just the flu
making me puke.
I wish so bad
that was true.

While I'm in
the bathroom,
I check again
for red
in my underwear,
hoping for blood,
but there are no
stains, except in
my brain, where
I imagine splashes
of menstruation,
shaped like angels
who save
my life.

Today I am seventeen.
Today I am half
of thirty-four.
Today I am
the old Sahara
no more.
I'm somebody new:
somebody
without a clue.

Mom made
a red velvet cake,
even though
she hates to bake,
and there are
seventeen pink candles.
There's also one
big white one,
for luck.

It sucks
when you can't even
eat cake
without hating
your life.
I fake a few bites,
pushing the white icing
to the side.

"You like?"
says Mom,
and I nod.
She's given me
an iPod.
It's a cool gift.
I'll download
some songs.
Probably all
sad songs:
Suicide Tunes.
Music to Kill
Yourself By.

I was surprised
when I unwrapped it,
because this
is a present
that a single parent
can't really afford.
Maybe she thought
that
I wouldn't act
so bored
if only I had an iPod
like
everyone else.

Emma
is the only one
at my sad little
party,
because I just wasn't
in the mood
for inviting.
I've been biting
everyone's head off.
Emma doesn't know
my dilemma.
How can I tell Emma,
whose family
is so Holy Roller?
Her life is the polar
opposite of mine.
What if she thinks
I'm going to hell?
What if she doesn't want
to hang out
with me:
the Knocked-Up Sleaze?
Her life is so easy.
Mine's not.

Emma's all dressed up
in black and white
polka dots,
and I'm feeling

like a frump
in a baggy T-shirt
and pajama bottoms.

"You look hot,"
says Curt to Emma.

"Polka dots
are a good look for you,"
says Mom.

"Minnie Mouse-ish
yet cute,"
says Heather.

Nobody ever says
that I look cute.
Maybe I should just
wear my clown suit.

"So, Sahara,
I'm taking you away
for your present,"
Emma says.

"What is it?" I ask.
"Is the gift
a trip?"

"Well, just down
to the Nail Palace,"
Emma says.
"I'm giving you
a manicure
and a pedicure."

It's too bad
that Emma
can't give me
a Baby-Cure, too.

"I think I'll choose
the nail color
blue,
to match my mood,"
I say
on the way
to the salon.

Emma just got
her license,
and she's driving
her Mom's Honda.
People keep beeping
because of the
bumper sticker
that says,
"Honk if you love Jesus."

Emma has good etiquette,
so she keeps beeping
back.

"I'm going to tell you
something wacked,"
I say to Emma.
I take a big breath.
"I'm pregnant."

"WHAT?"
Emma slams
on the brakes,
and she's shaking.
She takes my hand.
"Sahara, are you serious?"

"I wouldn't joke
about something
like this.
Are you pissed?
Do you hate me now?
I don't even know how
this happened to me.
I used to be so together,
Emma.
Now I'm a mess.
You don't have to be my friend
anymore,

now that you know
I'm such
a whore."
"Sahara!"
Emma pulls the car
to the side
of the street,
and she says something
so sweet
that I'll never
forget it.

"You are my friend
forever," she says.
"And I'd love
to baby-sit that kid.
If it's anything
like you,
I know I'll love it,
too."

I just squeeze
her hand,
because I can't
stand
to tell
my religious best friend
that I don't yet
know

if I'll let this kid
live
or if I'll just
Take Care Of It.

Pink Floyd's
"Comfortably Numb"
is like a mink
coat bundled
around my brain,
playing in my ear,
deadening
my head.

Next on the play list
is Led Zeppelin:
"Dazed and Confused."
That's my theme
song lately.
I'm the poster girl
for Dazed and Confused.
I feel so used:
Not only by Dustin,
but by myself.
After Led Zeppelin
comes the Stones:
"Wild Horses."

I wish that I could ride
a wild horse,
right out of this
life
and into
somebody else's.
Somebody not pregnant.
Somebody not numb.
Somebody not as dumb
as I've turned out
to be.

The nativity scene
is on top of our TV,
and the lights
on the tree
twinkle and blink
as I hunch,
blubbering,
over the bubbling sink
washing dishes.

My wish is
that I still
believed
in Santa Claus,
because back then
the world was filled

with magic.
Now it just seems tragic.
Why can't I wash
my troubles,
like bubbles,
down a drain?
Spray the pain
away so that
I'm left clean,
the way I
used to be.

Soon,
I won't
be able
to hide
what's inside
of me.

I need to decide,
and the choice is mine:
what will I do
about the pink line?

I pray for a sign.
Mother Mary was lucky.
An angel came.
She didn't have
to play this game.

It's so lame:
the way girls today
have to make
the Big Decision.

Three options:
Adoption,
Keeping,
or Leaping
into a place that
we can't see
with the end
of Planet Pregnancy.

It's Christmas-freaking-Eve,
and I can't believe
that I still haven't worked
up the nerve
to break the news.

I'm such a loser.
I deserve to be ostracized
for the rest of my life.
I deserve to never be
anybody's wife, or
anybody's daughter,
or anybody's sister.

Most of all,
I'm so not fit
to be somebody's mother.

I think that I'll be a recluse.
A loser of a hermit person
who lives in a dirty
falling-down old house
on a cold mountain,
with thirty thousand
stinking cats for company.
I'll be frumpy
and grumpy
and lumpy
in my stomach.

I'll eat stale dumplings,
and I just won't bother
with the outside world.

I'll wear the same
old-lady housedress
for eight days
in a row.

I'll wear no deodorant.
I'll have No Trespassing
signs, and lines
around my eyes
from crying.

No guys in my life.
Just me …
And maybe …
a baby.

This feels surreal.
Is it possible
that somebody could steal
the *real* me
and leave a
girl with an unplanned pregnancy
in my place?

I gaze
at my stranger's face
in a silver disco
Christmas ball
spinning from
the ceiling
of the mall.
My eyes are puffy
from crying,

and my hair's flying,
frizzy.
I'm dizzy.

Everybody seems busy
but me.
Everybody's with a family
except me.
Everybody seems happy.
Not me.

"Jingle Bells" is blaring,
and I'm not caring
about anything.

Santa's in his chair,
and I stare,
remembering how it felt
to be a little kid
on his knee.

"Silent Night"
is playing,
and Santa's elves
are swaying.
I wonder if they're drunk
or if they're just
touched
by the song.

Would it be wrong
for somebody
as big as me
to sit
on Santa's knee?
I just want to be
carefree.
I want to be
a little kid again.

There's no line,
because anybody
not a
depressed procrastinator
like me
has already seen
Santa
to put in their
requests.

I take a breath
and smooth my mess
of hair.
I don't care.
I'm going to do it.
Screw it.
I'm going to go
see Santa Claus.
There are no laws

against that.
It doesn't matter
if I'm fat.

"Hi, Santa," I say.
"Remember me?
Sahara Jane Searl?
You haven't seen me
since I was a little girl."

"Oh, Sahara!"
says Santa.
"You're on my list.
You're one
of the good kids."

Yeah, right.

"So, what do you want
for Christmas?"
Santa asks.
I perch on
his knee,
and Santa's eyes
are surprised,
but he's nice.

"Well," I say.
"I want a Lexus,
and I want to get out
of Texas."

"Ho, ho, ho! That's
a pretty big wish!"
Santa says. "How about something
small,
like a doll baby?"

"No," I say.
"Anything but a baby.
Maybe just
a regular life.
I want to be a normal teen.
Maybe you could
bring me
a magic fairy wand
to wave:
one that would take
me back
to the good old days."

"Okay!" says Santa.
"Ho, ho, ho!"

An elf clicks a picture.
I know it won't be
a good photo of me.
Pictures don't lie
even though I might.

"You have a good year, Sahara.
See you next Christmas."

I buy the picture
and glance at it
as I walk
away from Claus.
Who's that stranger
on Santa's lap?
I look like crap.

I wish I had a map
of the mall
because I can't decide
which direction
to walk.
It's Christmas-freaking-Eve,
and I can't believe
that I haven't bought
one single Christmas gift.

An annoying voice
chirps geekily
over the speakers:
"We will be closing
at ten o'clock!
Please finish
your shopping!
Happy, happy holidays!"

Yeah, right.
Bite me, bodyless voice.
I bet that you
never made one bad choice
in your mall-employed life.

I can't believe
that I'm still in the mall,
hauling ass,
walking fast past
a baby place,
tears lacing
my face.

It must be
all that pastel
yellow and green,
and blue and pink,
I think.

"Babies R Us"
has suddenly become
"Babies R Me."

Bummer.
By summer, maybe,
if I keep the baby,
I'll be a customer.

No more Hot Topic.
No more Deb Shop.
No more Old Navy,
except for the baby.

Just stuff for the baby,
and nothing for me.

That's what being a mother
means.

But I'm not a mother yet,
so I'm going to get
some cool new jeans
and they'll be
just for me:
A Christmas gift
from me to me,
to wear on
Planet Pregnancy.

I'm walking home
from the mall,
hauling a big pink
Victoria's Secret bag
of chintzy little gifts,
like a crazy Saint
Nicholas.

I bought underwear for Mom.
A leopard-print cell-phone cover
for Heather.
The new "Jackass" DVD for Curt.
A leather necklace for Emma.

The moon is full,
and stars sparkle,
trying to hark
Herald angels to sing,
I think.

Glory to the newborn King.
Peace on earth and mercy mild.
It was all about a newborn child.

I wonder if those three
wise men
felt as lost
as I feel now,

on this night.
I wish that a light
would guide me.
It's not fair
that *I* don't get
my own guiding
star.
How did those
Wise Men rate?
It's just my
destined fate,
I guess,
and just another
unfairness
in my mess
of a Half-Dead
Life.

Wearing my new
Army green
size 11 jeans
(because I threw
the old pants
in the trash can
of the mall bathroom),
I'm trying to pretend
that everything
is normal again.

I'm only seventeen.
This can't be
all left up to *me*.

Just because
I made one
big mistake
and gave away
my virginity,
for all infinity,
nothing
will ever again
be the same.

Everything
will change,
and the choice
I choose
will make
the difference
between
Keep,
Give Away,
or Lose.

A homeless
man who reeks
of booze
huddles on the corner

outside of the bank.
He's creepy,
and I get
the heebie-jeebies.
What if I
got raped?

Hey! That would make
a great lie.
An alibi
for why
I'm pregnant.
Or maybe
I could make
it a date rape!
Blame it on some
fake name that
Mom doesn't know.

This is a stroke-
of-genius plan,
and I have a freaking
reeking homeless
man to thank.

It's Christmas morning,
and crumpled wrapping paper
is all over the floor.

"I always feel so bad
for the poor
kids who don't
get gifts," Heather says.

She's on this big kick
of being Ms. Philanthropist.
Ms. Do-Gooder.
Ms. I Donate to the Disadvantaged.
It's funny
because we're not exactly
upper-income.
We're not bums,
but we're sure not rich.
We're kind of middle-income,
I guess.
We don't dress
in designer stuff.
Our biological father
never sees us
or supports us with money,
so it's kind of funny
that Heather's acting like
she lives in Paris Hilton's family.

She took gifts
to the Salvation Army
and to the soup kitchen,
and she mailed toys

to three little boys
in Iraq.
"They're poor.
They're living in the midst of war.
They sleep on the floor."
That's all she talks about anymore:
The Poor. The Disadvantaged.
Those in Pain.
She's insane.
She needs to take a look
in her own kitchen,
at her own sister:
the sibling
who's fibbing
every minute
of every day.

I'm gargling
with Listerine,
trying to hide
my throw-up breath.
I wish Heather would
just shut up
about her new boyfriend
Seth.
I look like death.

The Christmas tree is dying,
and I'm getting ready
to begin lying.
Is it a big sin
to tell a fib
at the most holy
time of the year?
It's not like I fear
getting struck by lightning
or growing a huge nose.
No.
God doesn't work like that.
He's an understanding guy.
He's forgiving.
He'll let me get away
with one tiny lie.

I'm vacuuming pine
needles from the floor.
This is like abortion, I think.
Suctioning stuff
that you don't want
out of a place where you don't
want it.
How easy would it be
just to call a pregnancy place
and make an appointment?
"Sahara Searl. Monday.

December 28th. 8:00 a.m."
Those few words could
make it all end.

I turn off the vacuum.
I leave the living room.
I find the phone book.
I look up the number.
I fumble with the phone.
"Hell—hello."
I'm stuttering.
My stomach's fluttering.
How can I just have someone
suck
a baby out of me?
I hang up.
I get back to vacuuming.
Pine needles
are not a fetus.

Dr. Proctor,
my annoying orthodontist,
is adjusting
my braces.

"Honestly," he says,
"you are going to have
a Miss America smile

when this is finished.
A Hollywood smile!
You'll be like Anna Nicole Smith!"

"She's dead," I mumble.
He fumbles around
in my mouth.

Dr. Proctor's breath
smells like cigarettes.
There should be a law
against dentists
who smoke.

"Gaining a little
bit of weight,
I see," says Dr. Proctor.
"Must be that new pizza
place: Carini.
Better watch out,
or you won't fit into
a bikini!"

I'm offended.
It's not his business
to notice
my weight
or anything below
my teeth.

I don't answer him.
"Don't forget
to wear the bands
at night. It'll help
your bite," he says.

I ignore him.
It's good
that Mom's insurance
pays for him
because he's not worth
my money
or my time
or my smile.
In a little while,
crooked teeth
will be the least
of my worries.

I can't believe this,
but I'm completely
crushing, in lust.
There's a new family
renting the rust-colored
house next door,
and they have one son.

This is a surprise.
You'd think that I'd
be finished—done—
with guys.

He has green eyes,
and shaggy black
hair.

I allow myself
to stare
as he skateboards,
crouched down,
low to the ground.
I don't care.
I just stare.

He's hot.
I'm not.
Mother Nature
should make
pregnant girls
get nauseous
and cautious
when guys
with green eyes
are nearby.

It doesn't happen,
though.
Instead,
I gag
at meat and eggs
and even peaches.

I envision leeches
on the neighbor,
doing myself a favor,
hoping to gross
myself out.

It doesn't work.
I lurk
behind the curtain,
certain
that he
would never
look twice
at a not-nice
girl
like me.

Mom's in a bad mood,
but it's time to tell
her about the make-believe
Dude.

I'm almost starting
to believe my own lie:
The Great Date Rape.

I hate the guy.
I've named
him Blake.
Blake of the Great
Date Rape.
He's the bad guy.
I'm innocent.
I'm the victim.
I wish I'd kicked him
in the testicles
rather than getting
pregnant.
I wish I'd used self-defense.
I wish I'd had common sense.
I never should have dated Blake.
That boy sure can make
a fool out of a girl
who's a virgin.
The surgeon general
should issue warnings
about horny boys
like Blake.
They can cause pregnancy
and other diseases.

"Mom," I say, "I have
to tell you something.
It happened, like, about
five months ago.
I know
I should have told you then,
when it first
happened.
It's something crappy.
It's not going to make you happy."

Mom's preoccupied.
She's thinking about bills.

"How would you feel
if I took birth control pills?"
I ask.
I'm an ass.
This was unplanned
and a bad idea.

"Why the hell
would you need
birth control pills?!"
Mom's spazzing.

"I ... I don't," I say.
This is the truth.
It's too late,

after Blake and the Great
Date Rape.

"Um, there's this guy
who goes to Allenwood High," I say.
"His name is Blake.
His eyes are like a
blue lake. Fake.
He wears colored contacts
and always dresses in black.
He's whacked.
He smokes
and drinks,
and I think
he does drugs.
He slugs
guys in other gangs!"

Mom pushes up her bangs
and stares at me.
"You hang
with gangs?"
she asks.

"No!" I say.
"Just one day,
I went on a little date.
A date,
with Blake."

Mom's eyes are on fire.
I wonder if she knows that
I'm a liar.
"And why
wouldn't you tell
me about this guy?
You could've been
killed, Sahara!
That was a stupid
move. A lunatic
thing to do.
He could have
hurt you!"

"He did," I say.
"He, like, raped me, Mom."

Mom explodes.
She slams her hands
on the table.
"Where does he live?
Who are his parents?
What's his last name?
Did you call the police?
Did you go to the doctor
or the hospital?
Did you have any tests?"

"I'm not pregnant," I say.
"I'm fine.
He moved away,
and I don't even know
his last name.
Blake moved to New York.
He's a dork, anyway.
Please calm down, Mom.
We don't need the police.
I don't have a disease."

Unless you count
a baby inside of me
or a really bad case
of lying about a date rape
by a guy named Blake.

I'm looking at my
baby book.
Mom did
a good job
of keeping up
for a couple
of years.
It ended, though,
when I was four.
She's recorded
stuff about my umbilical cord,

my first bath,
a little cut on my hand.
She wrote
about doctor appointments
and diaper-rash ointment,
immunizations, and our very
first vacation.
That was before
she and my dad
divorced.

It's weird thinking
of our family including
a father.
It's always been
just
Mom and me,
Curt, and Heather …
for as long
as I can remember.
I was born in December,
and they separated in May.
I had a dad
for one hundred and eighty days.
There's proof
in these pictures:
the ancient history
of our family.

They really loved me.
They saved pieces
of me:
locks of blonde hair,
teeny baby teeth,
a dried-up
old belly-button
stump,
tiny fingernail clippings.
Tears are slipping
down my face,
because it has just hit me:
This baby inside of me
has pieces of me,
too.
I try
not to cry,
and I close the book.
It's better
if I just don't look,
or think,
or feel.
I make a
private deal
with myself:
Just put the baby book
back on the shelf.

Somebody had
a baby in the toilet
and it drowned.
The criminal's picture
is on the Internet.
She was wearing a
purple prom gown
covered with blood.

Somebody else
gave birth in a hotel,
and I think she'll go to hell,
because she just shoved
that new baby
into a black trash bag
and threw it
into a blue Dumpster.

Another moron idiot
stuck an infant
in a blanket
and left it
in the trunk of her car
while she went
into a bar
and got drunk.
What a punk.
The baby died,

and she's being tried
for murder.

There's a law
about how
you can't get in trouble
for dumping your baby
at a hospital or a fire station
or a church,
as long as you do it
within something like three days
after birth.
For what it's worth,
I'm not thinking about doing that.
I couldn't deal
with how I'd feel.

The law
is called Safe Haven,
and it's a great thing,
but I couldn't bring
myself to drop off my kid
like a donation
to a fire station.

Mom and Heather
and Curt went
on a ski vacation

to Pennsylvania.
It was paid for
by Mom's work,
as a reward
for her being on some
trustees' board.

"I just need to get away," Mom said.
"I can't even begin to deal
with you being raped, Sahara.
I'm on the verge
of a nervous breakdown.
My stomach's in knots,
and I'm seeing dots—
floaters—in my right eye.
Good-bye."

Why, oh why,
does my mother
always have to make everything
all about *her?*
Her knots; *her* dots?
What about *my* stomach?
What about *my* eyes,
ugly from crying
all the time?
She acts as if
I'm the one
who committed a crime.

I lied
about a fake rape.
I've turned my mom into a mental
patient.
I don't deserve a vacation.
I didn't go.
I'm at home alone.
I used the excuse
of having the flu,
which isn't far
from the truth.
And now here I sit,
surfing the 'net,
reading sick articles
about sick psychos
who do crazy things
to babies.
Psychiatrists say
that they
are in denial.
Maybe I'm in denial, too,
because I can't even begin
to think about
what to do.
Denial is not beautiful.
Denial is a nonhelpful thing.

I've done it.
I've made the
Appointment.
I'm going to
Take Care
Of It.

I'm scared shitless.

It's late Saturday
afternoon,
and the moon
is already
in the sky.

Is the moon
confused, too?

I'm crying
as I drive.
I can't help it.
I can't stop.
I'm sobbing.

The world
is a blur.
My tongue is
fur.

I'm detached
from my body,
and I can't
believe
that this is Me.

I'm on my way
to get rid of
a baby.

It's kind of late
in the pregnancy.

I've seen
those pictures
of what's inside
of me.

I'm a horrible,
sorry
excuse
for a human being.

I don't deserve
to live.

I wish it was the
other

way around.
I wish that
the baby-to-be
could abort
Me.

It has a heart that beats.
It has feet
and toes.

I know
it has eyes
and a nose
and a mouth
to suck
its thumb.
I know it's more
than just
a nothing, and
I know that
this is wrong.

I'm shivering,
quivering,
all over.

Will this hurt?
What do they do
with the stuff

that's sucked
out of a womb?
Is there a room
for Aborted Babies?

What if it
haunts me
like a ghost?

Will I recover?
Will I ever have a real
Baby
And be a real
Mother?

I'm not alert,
and I'm not
exerting the
defensive driving
skills that I learned
in driver's ed.

I'm out of my head,
out of my body,
out of my mind.
I've left Sahara
behind,
in my old life.

I'm flying,
fast,
Chuck Taylor sneaker
pressed
hard on the gas.
Fast. Fast.

I'm leaning
over the steering
wheel,
careening
down a hill.
I don't want
to feel.

Is this minute real?

My knuckles are white
on the wheel.

Colors whiz by.
They fill my head.
There's red.
It's a Stop sign.
I do not stop.
Crashing, smashing, bashing.
A van smacks
the front fender.

The world spins.
I close my eyes.
"Why didn't you stop?"
There's a cop.

It must have been God.

I'll be getting a ticket.
My car's messed up.

I'm still breathing.
My heart is beating.

I was wearing my seat
belt, and I felt
it when I was hit.
Shit.
I hope that the baby
is okay.

I tell the officer.
"I'm pregnant."
He doesn't know me.

"The air bag
could have deployed."
The cop is annoyed.
"You should go to
the hospital."

"I'm okay."
I don't know
what else to say.

"Your insurance rates
will go through the roof,"
says the cop.

"Okay," I say.

I'm going home.
I can still drive.
I hope that the baby
will survive.

This is a sign.

I'm dialing
Mom's cell-
phone number,
getting ready
to bum her out
on her ski trip.

She's going to flip
about my accident.

I get her voice mail
recording, which she's
changed to say,
"Hi! This is Stephanie!
I'm skiing and hopefully
not breaking any bones,
so I'll phone
you back.
Leave a message, please,
at the beep!"

Her voice is so cheery
it's fake.

I take
a breath
and let my
message
out fast:
"Hey, it's me.
I had a tiny
fender bender.
Nothing major.
I drove home.
I'm fine.
Bye."

In less than
a minute,
she calls back
and she's wacked
out.

"Sahara! What in
the world
did you do?
Do you have any
clue how expensive
your insurance will be?"

"The cop told me," I reply.
"It'll be
through the roof."

"Well, you're paying it.
Not me.
I'm not about to be
the one
paying for your
mistakes."

"Okay."

"Now you'll
have points
on your record,

too. Don't be
all blue
when you lose
your license,
young lady."

"Okay."

"Is that all
you have to say?" Mom yells.

"Yes," I say.

I've had way
enough stress
in this mess
of a day,
so I just
hang up,
and I wonder
if mothers
are allowed
to ground
pregnant daughters
for life.

It's New Year's Eve,
and I can hardly believe

that a brand-new year
could hold
so much old
fear.
Dustin is here,
and Curt is burping
beer.

It's almost
twelve o'clock,
and Dick Clark's Rockin'
New Year's Eve
show is on.

"Countdown!" says
Dustin, clowning around.
People on TV
are wearing glittery gowns,
which makes me
feel down somehow.
I'm a cow.

How can I tell
Dustin, who's always
bustin' on his cousin
for getting pregnant?

Dustin's too young
and dumb.

He's a bum.
He doesn't work.
He's a jerk.
He'd be
a bad dad,
just like the dad
I never had.

It's 11:59,
in the Year
of the Pink Line.

At the stroke
of midnight
I fight the urge
to regurgitate
when my date
kisses my cheek.
He's a geek.
How could I be
so weak
to let Dustin
impregnate
me?

The ball drops
in Times Square,
and I don't even care.

I just stare
at the TV screen,
leaving behind
the Year of the Pink Line,
and hoping
that I'll be coping
just fine
at this time
next year.

Emma's always at
basketball practice,
and so
my bed
is my best
friend.
It's one
place
that feels
safe,
so I just
stay in it
all day.
I can't
stop crying.
I'm dying
inside.

My eyes
are puffed,
and my nose is
totally stuffed.
I can't get enough
air, but I don't
really care.

I guess
that I'm depressed,
because breath
doesn't seem necessary
even if it means
death.

I'm wacked.
Maybe I need
Prozac.

I see black
through the cracks
of my blinds,
and realize
that it's night.

I bite my nails,
and wonder
what would happen
if I just bailed

out of this jail
called Life.

Suicide lies
undisguised,
lurking in my mind.
But with my
dumb luck,
death
would suck, too.

School is so
not cool.
The teachers
are geeks,
and the weeks
drag like rags
through mud.
School is
crud.
At this time
next year,
I'll still be here,
waiting to graduate
in gown and cap
into the Real World
of crap.

I wonder
if I'll be a mother
then?
If you're a mom,
can you still
go to the prom?

I'm in Family Living,
where the teacher is giving
a lecture
on sex and pregnancy.
I feel like
everybody's
looking at me,
even though nobody
knows.

Yesterday,
I totally
broke up
with Dustin.
He's disgusting.
How could
I have ever
been in lust
with Dustin?

I didn't bother
to tell him that
he's the father
of the Embryo.
He called me
a "ho,"
so I don't
want him to
know
anything about me
or the baby.

The genetics
are pathetic
when it comes
to Dustin.

I'll just tell
the kid
that I bid
on e-Bay
and won.

Or that the stork
was a dork,
and the delivery
was made by
mistake
to me.

Or maybe
I'll just
go
for the termination again
and pretend
that it's a vacation,
relieving the
conceiving
with one big suck
of all the muck
of the past months.

Or with
the option
of adoption,
the kid
could just live
somewhere else,
with a family
much less confused
than me.

Family living
isn't all it's
cracked up
to be.

I'm in church
learning about sinners
and saints
and feeling like I could
faint.

Is this hypocritical
or ridiculous:
me,
being here
as if premarital
sex is
a mystery
to me?

I'm wearing a long
gauze
hippie skirt,
purple and green,
because it has a
stretchy waistband.
Emma drew a henna
tattoo on my hand,
a pattern
of fancy flowers
and swirls
for a wedding.
I'm betting

that I'll never
have a wedding.

There's a young couple
huddled close together
in the pew ahead.
Their shoulders touch,
and they look like
a team.
This is what a baby
needs:
two people.
A mother,
and a father.
Why bother
to try to raise
a baby
when there's not
a whole
family?

I consider
whispering
to the couple:
How would you two
like to adopt
a baby in a few
months?
You look like

you could be
good parents.

I don't do it,
though,
because I just know
that the answer
would be no.
What if Father Shawn,
who's been my priest
for at least sixteen years,
knew about this?
He'd be pissed.
He'd be disappointed.

Maybe I should just quit
being a Catholic
if it means being
a hypocrite?
No. I'm not a bad ass.
I deserve to come to Mass.
I just made a mistake.
Even political people
and celebrities from TV
screw up sometimes.
They are just like me.
I wonder
if ending a pregnancy
is a bigger sin

than any other.
I'm not ready
to be a mother.

Cupid is stupid,
and Valentine's Day
is way
lame.

It's all a game:
posers with roses
and hearts
and cards
that tell lies.

It's no surprise
that I didn't get
anything from
anybody.

I take some
money
from my bunny
bank,
and I crank
up the radio
in my faded,
outdated,

smashed-up
Toyota Celica,
listening to
Metallica
as I drive
to the Five and
Dime.

It's no crime
to buy yourself
a valentine,
and so I get
the largest
red heart
of chocolates.

The sales clerk
is way too perky,
and kind of jerky.

"These are discounted
fifty percent!" she says.
"Nifty! Fifty percent is
nice. If you want my
advice, it makes sense
to buy Valentine's gifts
at night because the
candy goes on sale!"
Great. I know how *I* rate.

This lady's on to me.
I have no date, and so I
wait until late
to buy myself
a cheap box
of chocolates.

I hate love,
and Cupid
sucks.

On President's Day,
Ms. Hay,
the lesbian
history teacher,
is preaching,
lecturing
about presidents,
especially her own
personal favorite:
Abe Lincoln.

I'm yawning,
just trying to
stay awake,
as Ms. Hay
yaks about
Abe.

Maybe I
should've been
a lesbian, I'm
thinking, because
then there'd be
no stinking
pink line.
Everything would
be fine.
The benefits
of lesbianism
are now
obvious.
Gay Ms. Hay
will never get
pregnant, at
least not
by the regular
method.

"Baby Abe
was adored,
even though
his family
was poor,"
Ms. Hay states.

I catch my breath
because I never

thought of a President
as ever being a baby.
That's crazy, to think
that my Egg
could one day
be President.

My Coast-soap
Embryo might
cure AIDS someday.
It might
cure cancer.

She could be
a dancer
in a fancy frou-frou
tutu.
He could be
the next pope.

The Coast soap
has hope.

It's a he
or a she,
and has
its own
personal
history.

I'm in
the baby department
at Wal-Mart
pushing an empty
cart. It's not smart
to be seen
in this section,
but it's just such
a confection
of soft and silky,
pink and green and blue.

I'm hoping
that if I just touch
some of this stuff,
it'll help convince
me what to do.
Maybe a baby
will seem like a real
Thing,
if I can just
bring
myself to buy
one teeny-tiny
sweater.

But then
a lady

with a
wailing baby
in a sling
brings a big commotion
of noise
down the aisle.
She's singing,
and she
makes crazy faces,
trying to make
the baby happy.
It doesn't work.
Her stupid song
is a big waste
because that red-faced
baby
just keeps crying.
The mom is trying,
but nothing works.

I'm annoyed.
This is so much
noise.
I want the kid
to shut up.
I push my cart
right out
of that department
and into the movie display,

where no big-mouth baby
is taking my
sanity away.

An economy box
of Kotex
feminine protection
takes up a section
of my closet:
a deposit
for the future.
I never imagined
that I'd ever
miss the Curse.

I wonder if I'll nurse?
Something sucking
on my boobs
would be lewd.
It'd probably hurt.
I don't think I'll nurse.

But I'd probably
overheat the bottles
in the bottle warmer.
Then I'd waste my paycheck
buying more formula.
That stuff costs an

arm and a leg,
just to feed
the Egg.

I guess
I should check
into WIC.
It's like welfare,
and people will stare,
but why should
I care?

I wonder where
you go to get WIC?
I'm not a hick.
I don't pick my nose.
I'm not toothless …
just clueless
as to how in the heck
I'm going to survive
when I have to buy
all the supplies
for an extra life.

You need
diapers and wipes,
a crib, bibs, nipples
for bottles and the liquid
that goes inside.

You need
a car seat, and a thing
to heat the milk,
and blankets.

What if the kid's
cranky? What if it
has colic
and won't stop
crying? I'll be
buying medicine,
like Ritalin, for
kids who are hyper.
What if I can't
afford enough diapers?

You need stuff
like cough syrup
and a thermometer
and a monitor
so you can hear
the kid no matter
where you go.

You need clothes
and shoes and all kinds
of pink and blue
and yellow and green
that the kid will

grow out of,
and then you'll need
to buy more stuff.
You need
a little hairbrush
and a pacifier
to hush
the kid up.

You need
little nail clippers
and sippy cups
and fluffy pups
that make music
when you
wind them up.

You need onesies
and books about
bunnies.
You need
a stroller
and a folding
playpen
for when
you can afford
to go away.

You need a
diaper bag
and baby cream
for diaper rash
and mashed-up
bananas.

You need
powder and
Ivory Snow
to wash the clothes.

You need
Baby Magic
to wash
the kid.
You need
lids for little
plastic dishes
of Cheerios.

You need
a teeny spoon
with a coating
and boats
and rubber ducks
and beads
for the baby
to bite

when it's
getting a new
tooth.

You have to be
the Tooth Fairy
and Santa Claus
and the Easter Bunny,
while the kid
has all the fun
and gets all
the money.

You need
a changing table
and cable TV
for *Sesame Street*.

You need
to protect
the kid
from electricity
by sticking
plugs in
outlets.
You need
to put stuff
up on a shelf
so the

kid doesn't
break it.

You need
to get up
at night.

I need
my sleep.

You need
teeny T-shirts
and swimming
suits and snow
boots.

You need
lullabies
and small-size
jackets,
and a backpack
to carry
the kid
on your back.

It's a fact
that babies
die of crib death,
so you have to

watch their breath,
to make sure
that they're still
alive.
You can't let
them die.
You have to
keep them
alive.

You need
doctor appointments,
and ointments,
and shots,
and lots
of baby food.

You need
shoes again
and again
because the
kid keeps growing.

It never ends.

You need
music lessons
and dress-up clothes
for special events.

You need
a fence
or a gate
so they
don't fall
down steps
and break
their necks.

You need
a tiny toilet
for potty training,
and lots
of patience.

You have
to clean up
about three million
messy butts.

You need
to teach
the ABCs
and 1-2-3s,
and eventually
the birds
and the bees.

You need
to push the kid
on swings and
buy it swim wings
and sing
stupid songs
like "Ring Around
the Rosey"
and "Rock-A-Bye, Baby."

You need
to sit through
baseball games
and lame school plays,
and you never
get to be lazy.

You have to
play Candyland
and Chutes and Ladders.

But it doesn't matter,
because now you're
a mother.
You need
to buy animal crackers
and apple juice
and go to the zoo.

You have
to hang out
in the baby-ride section
of the amusement
park.

You have to bark
like a dog
and oink like a hog
when the kid
wants to pretend
to walk on four legs.

You have to hide
Easter eggs.

You need
educational toys,
and you can't
get annoyed
with all the noise.

You have
to go to cartoon movies,
and drive
like a mom:
paranoid of getting
hit because of
the kid.

You can't go
to the prom,
but the kid will
someday.

You need
to work overtime
for the rest
of your life
to pay for
all the stuff,
but it
still won't be
enough.
How will
I survive
and keep
me and the
kid alive?

Trimester Three

Forever Is Ahead

On Saint Patrick's
Day I decide
that it's time
to drop the bomb.
I'm going to tell Mom.

I chose this date
because of Irish luck.
I'm obviously fucked up
because we have
no Irish blood
whatsoever.
Dustin does,
so the Egg
is a tiny bit
Irish.
Maybe the baby
is a leprechaun.
I pray
that it in no way
resembles
its sperm donor,
Dustin the Boner.
I searched
all over
the yard
for a four-leaf
clover
or some green,

any green,
but all I found
were weeds,
all brown.

This brought
me down.
Maybe the brown
was an omen,
a sign of an
explosion
from My Mother,
the Spaz.

She's going
to freak.

I feel weak.
I think I'm
going to barf.

Mom's wearing
a green scarf.
She never forgets
a holiday.
She also never forgets
a mistake.
My Mom expects
perfection, especially

in her offspring.
I'm cracking
my knuckles
and gnawing
my nails,
as Mom
paints her perfect
nails with green
sparkle.

"Eat a good
breakfast," Mom says.
She thinks
that pancakes and eggs
can solve all the problems
of the world.

My stomach
is in a curl.
I'm going to
hurl.

"I have
something
to tell you,"
I stammer.
My heart
is a hammer.

"Sahara,"
says Mom,
"did you fail
your French test?"

Non, ma mère.
I failed
the EPT test,
I must confess.
That's worse
than all the other tests
put together.

"Worse," I say.
"Worse than
flunking French."
Why can't I
just say the words:
"I'm pregnant"?

"Oh, Lord," Mom says.
"Science again?"

"Worse." It sounds
like a curse.

"Just tell me, Sahara.
I'm going to be late
for work."

I'm such a jerk.
The words are stuck
in my stomach,
along with the Egg.
I guess the Egg
is now more than just
an egg.
I guess it's now officially
a Fetus.

I take a breath.
This sentence
might mean death.

"I'm having a baby."
My blubber
jiggles as I wiggle
in the kitchen chair.
"I'm pregnant.
I'm sorry. I'm really,
really sorry, Mom."

Mom's face drains.
I'm having labor pains.
This feels so not real.
Mom's going to keel
over. Her four-leaf
clover scarf didn't bring
luck. This sucks.

I'm killing
my mother.

"Who's the father?"
Mom asks, her face
a mask.

I debate.
I hate him.
Should I tell
Mom that it's
Dustin?
He's disgusting.

"It doesn't matter," I say.
"I don't want him
to know."

Mom explodes.
"That is so
irrational, Sahara.
You need
support!"

Not if I abort.
"We'll take him
to court," Mom says.
"Get an attorney."

Mom thinks that
the legal system
can fix anything.
It can't fix this.
I'm pissed.

"The father's a jerk!
I'll work.
I'll work two jobs,
or I'll rob
banks. He's a skank.
I don't want the baby
to be like him.
No, thanks.
I can do it alone.
I'll get a loan."

Mom groans.
"You have no concept
of what's ahead.
You're heading
down a long, hard road,
young lady,
if you plan
on raising a baby
alone."

134

"I know," I say.
"But it's not impossible.
You did a good job."

Mom starts
to sob.

"I'll get a job," I say.
"Don't worry, Mom."

My mom has crumpled,
and thanks to me,
she's now nothing
but one
big lump
of worry.

I'm eating salami
and watching news
about a huge tsunami
in Asia.
Babies are dead, swept away
by a tidal wave.
Others are left
without parents:
sad orphans mourning.
They can't even talk.
They can't walk.

My baby swims
in the Sea of Me,
safe from tsunami waves.
I don't want it to come out.
It's too dangerous
out here.
I don't care if you're in
the United States of America
or in Asia
or in Transylvania,
there's too damn much danger.
No wonder Mary kept Jesus
in the manger.
There are strangers who
kidnap babies.

There are tsunami waves
that sweep them away.
There are airplanes
that crash into buildings.
The news is beginning
to panic me.

I just want to build
a canopy over my baby
and keep it from all the bad stuff.
It's been through enough,
with the rough start that I gave it.
I already suck as a mother.

Mom comes into the living room.
"Maybe it'd be best
to think about adoption," she says,
right out of the blue.
"I don't know if you
are ready for this responsibility.
Don't expect me
to raise this baby.
I've raised three kids.
I'm finished.
I'm done.
I'm too tired to begin
again."

I just stare at the TV screen.
Mom is so freaking mean.
I hate her.
She hates me.
She hates the baby.

"Look at all the babies in Asia,"
Mom says.
"Phone calls are pouring in
from people who want to adopt them.
There are families out there
who'd give an arm and a leg,
desperate
to get a healthy infant.
Wealthy families with the means

to give a baby
everything it needs."

She's so freaking mean.
"Sahara," Mom says,
"you have no clue."

I do.
I have a clue.
She's the one who knows nothing.
She sucks as a mother.

I'm at Emma's
perfect house,
eating dinner
with her perfect
Holy Roller
family.
They say grace.
They never waste
food
because of starving
children in China.
They use fine china,
and they are
polite.
They don't fight
at meals

or at night.
Their furniture
is white.

After dinner,
Emma and I
sit on the
snow-colored
sofa.
Emma has the remote.

"Let's watch
that show
about plastic surgery,"
I suggest.
"It's the best show."

"No," Emma says.
"Beauty is on the inside.
I don't like that
show."

I know better
than to argue
with Emma.
It's her TV.
She's holding the remote,
not me.
I'm just hoping

that she doesn't decide
that we need
to watch one of
those TV preachers,
or somebody teaching
you how to decorate.
I hate
Emma's taste
in television.

"How about
'What Not To Wear?'"
I say.

"No way," Emma says.
"I don't care
what other people
say not to wear."

"But they even do hair!"

"I don't care."

We both stare at the
TV screen.
Emma points the remote.
She surfs and clicks,
but then she stops
at something sick.

It's a lady
in labor.
"Change it!" I say.

"I love this stuff!" Emma whispers.
"It's a miracle. It's so cool.
Just think, Sahara. Soon
that will be you."

"Great. I can't wait."
The lady's face
is twisted,
and her hands
are in fists.
She's pissed,
you can tell,
and she looks like
hell.
Sweating, eyes wild,
the lady is pushing
and yelling,
yelling and pushing.
I grab
the cushions of
the sofa.
The lady groans,
moaning.
The camera zooms
in on a place

that TV should never see.
"Gross," I say.
"Ewwwwww."

"That'll be you!" Emma says.
"Hey, there's the head!
It's crowning!"

The lady shouts.
The baby pops out,
and it's the most gross
thing on this earth:
slime and blood and stuff.
"That's enough.
I can't watch
another minute.
This is sick!"

I close my eyes
and put my fingers
in my ears
so that I can't hear.
"La, la, la, la, la," I say,
hoping to make it all
go away.

We're in a waiting room,
with a bunch of other

expectant wombs.
There's been a pregnancy
boom in Texas,
I can see,
mostly with girls
like me.
Mom's pretending
to read a magazine.
Her green nails
are chipped,
and she's biting
her lip.

My pants are unzipped.
The Fetus kicks.
I think it's pissed
because I didn't see
a doctor before this.

"Sahara," calls a nurse.
Mom lifts her purse.

"I can do this by myself," I say.
"I'm not a baby."

Mom follows me.
She's good at ignoring me.
She's also good
at acting really mad

at me and at making me feel
really guilty.
We go into a blue room
painted with rubber ducks
and beach buckets.
There's a table
with stirrups
and machines for seeing
inside of me.

I need to pee.
I had to drink
a sinkful of water
for this test.
My bladder flutters.
So does my stomach.

I'm scared.
I hate how this
ugly gown
doesn't cover
all of my parts,
and how I'm
breaking my mother's
heart.
I'm going to hear
the baby's heart.

I accidentally fart
when the nurse
rubs the gel
across my belly.

"Excuse me," I say.
I'm so embarrassed.

"That's okay.
I've seen and heard
everything," says the nurse.
"Modesty goes out
the window,
honey,
when it comes
to giving birth.
It's worth it,
though."
I don't know
about that.
This kid
better be worth
my getting fat.

The blue room
matches my mood,
and I'm trying
hard not to be rude.

"What is the doctor
going to do?" I ask.

"Make sure
that the baby
is okay."

Now my heart
breaks. What
if the baby
isn't okay?
What if I
have one of
those kids
with cleft lips,
or Down syndrome?
What if it's
mentally retarded,
and it's all
my fault
because I didn't
get medical care
soon enough?

What if all kinds
of stuff
is wrong
and the kid
has to live

with me
until we're both old
and making each other
crazy?

What if I didn't eat
right? What if the kid
got brain damage
in gym, when I did
somersaults?
It'll all be
my fault.
What if
it has webbed toes
or a smashed-in nose?
What if it never knows
its own name?
What if it's lame
and can't walk?
What if it can't talk?
What if it's deaf
or blind?
I'll blame myself
forever, and nothing
will ever
be right
again.

The shape
of my baby
is glistening
on the screen
of a machine,
and we
are listening
to the beat
of its heart.

I start
to weep,
and I know
that I'll keep
this kid,
no matter
how hard
it is.
The heartbeat
is part
of me,
and I'm
part
of it,
and we're
connected
by much more
than just

an umbilical cord.
Mom's eyes
are lined with red,
like a road map to nowhere.
She touches
my stomach.
I can't tell if she's mad
or sad
or depressed
or just making the best
of a bad situation.

"Is it a girl
or a boy?" Mom asks
the doctor.

"No!" I yell.
"Don't tell!
I want it to be
a surprise
when it comes
out.
Pregnancy is
all about
a gender-free
kind of love."

I remember
how I went

to Madam Mystic.
I must have
been psycho
to go to a psychic.
Maybe it
was the hormones.
Now I don't
want to know
the sex
of the baby
because I'm
in love,
no matter
what,
with this
heart that beats
inside of me,
regardless of
whether
it's a he
or a she.

My great-grandmother,
Mom's Granny Fran,
has died.
She was ninety-five.
I don't really cry
because I didn't

really know her.
She lived far away,
in a nursing home
in New York City.
Fran was so pretty
in an old picture
of Mom's,
and I thought it was
a pity
that people
change as they
age.

"What happened?" I ask.

"She lived
a long life,
full of joy
and heartache,"
Mom says.
"She lost
a newborn
son, and then
another, and then
an infant daughter."

My eyes start
to water.
"Three babies died?
Why?"

"Hard times," Mom replies.
"Crib death
was common
back then."

It makes me cry,
that Granny Fran's
three babies
died.
No baby
should have
a grave
before it
learns
to walk or talk
or write
its name.

I realize
something:
Now that
I've decided
to become a
mother,
nothing
will be the same …
not even an
unknown
dead baby's name

with two dates
on a gravestone.

Mom's leaving
on a kind of vacation
concerning Granny Fran's
cremation,
scattering the ashes
in Nashville.

It's Mom's job
because her parents
aren't in the States.
Mom's parents
ran away
to Jamaica,
where they're
escaping responsibility,
living in a trailer
by the sea.
I wish that was me.

Maybe I should just
run away.

I can't even believe
that Mom's mom
isn't flying back

to scatter her own *mother*.
She won't even bother
with anything that
doesn't come
with a Bob Marley
soundtrack
playing in the background.
Life isn't all about just kicking back
in Paradise,
you know.

Eventually
my so-called grandparents
will have to
grow up
and face
the Real World.
Mom hasn't even called
to tell them about me
and the Pregnancy.

I wish that I had
real grandparents
like Emma does:
the warm and fuzzy kind.
Emma's grandmother wears
sweaters and dresses,
not bikinis.
She drinks hot tea,

not tequila.
Emma's grandmother
doesn't listen to Bob Marley
or ride a Harley.

I really want
my baby to have
a traditional
rational
actual
grandmother
to love.
Maybe *my* mom
should take grandmother
classes
so that she knows
how to act
with the baby.
The great-granny
I never
knew
is burned,
in the urn,
in Mom's arm.
Mom puts it in
her car.
It's a far
drive
when you're

the only one
alive.
"Why are you taking
Granny Fran's ashes
to Nashville?"
Heather asks.

"Her big dream
was to be
a country
singing star,"
Mom says.
"She always
wanted to go
to Nashville.
You know,
she never got
farther south
than Asheville,
North Carolina.
So close
yet so far.
So now
I'm taking her there
in my car.
She'll finally
be a star."

"That's creepy,"
Heather says.
"This ashes thing
is freaking
me out.
They came
on a UPS truck,
in a box.
That's just weird,
and maybe even
illegal."

"It's okay," I say.
"Death is part of life."

Heather needs to grow up.
I guess
when you're carrying
the beginning of a new life
inside,
you don't hide
from the end of
a life, either.

"Say good-bye
to your great-
grandmother," Mom
says as she starts
the car.

This is crazy.
I never even knew
the lady.
The baby
inside of me
is *related*
to her.

"Wait!" I say
before Mom drives away.
"Can you just leave
a tiny piece
of her here
so that she's near?"

Mom shrugs
and then she
reaches out
and hugs me.

"That's a fine
idea," she says.
"A little bit of
Granny Fran
should be close to
her descendants."

Heather rolls her eyes,
and she and Curt

go inside.
They don't understand
about Granny Fran.
They aren't carrying
part of her
beneath *their*
hearts.

On Planet Pregnancy,
descendants
are a big deal.
My clueless brother and sister
don't know
how it feels
to have ancestors
matter.

Mom opens
the urn,
lifting
a tiny bit
of the remains
with her
fingertips.
They're gray.
No way
would I have
guessed that.

Mom sifts
a bit
into my hand.
They feel okay.
I take a breath,
and then I just let
them go.
Granny Fran
is lifted into
the air,
and some of her
lands
in my
hair.
I don't care.

Heather stares
from the
kitchen window,
but she
just doesn't
know.

The sky goes
suddenly darker,
and the wind whips.
It's blowing hard.
Thunder rumbles.

Mom starts to laugh.
"That's Granny Fran!"
she says.
"She always was one
to be spontaneous:
footloose and fancy-free.
She wants to be
here,
with us!
The hell with Nashville!"

I can't believe this:
My structured mother,
usually so uptight,
is acting on impulse
for the first time
in her life.
Maybe she's lost
her mind.
Maybe having
a pregnant teenage
daughter
makes a mother
go
crazy.

My hair's blown
across my face,
and Mom's skirt

is billowing around her,
like Marilyn Monroe
in that old movie
she loves.

"She's telling us
to just leave her here!"
Mom shouts over the
thunder.

She turns the urn
upside down,
and the ashes
snow down,
around us,
in Texas:
a wild blizzard
of a
related lady
my baby
will never
know.

My mother
has called
my father.
I'd rather
that she

didn't bother.
"Why'd he
have to know?"
I am so
annoyed
and way not
overjoyed.

"He is
your biological
father," Mom says.

"Bio, maybe.
Logical, no.
So what did
Bio-Dad say?"

"That the day
has arrived
for him to be
part of your
life," Mom announces.

I flounce
on the couch,
holding my pouch
of stomach.
"Why now?
Wow. All of

a sudden
the old dud
wants to
be a parent
to me?"

Mom shrugs.
She tugs on
her hair. I
stare at the
ceiling, not
sure of what
I'm feeling.

"So now
he's just
going to hop
on the grandpop
wagon, after all
these years
of slacking?
He must be
lacking a brain.
That's insane."
"Forgiving is
living without
bitterness," Mom
says. "Let go
of the past,

and give him
half a chance,
Sahara."

I sigh,
feeling weak.
What a geek
he must be.

But then again,
I bet that maybe
he's a lot
like me.

Bio-Dad
comes for
dinner.
He's no winner,
and I'd be a sinner
to lie
and say
that he's a super
guy. He eats
too much pie
and burps.

Curt snickers
when Bio-Dad

bickers
with Mom
about it being
good manners
to belch
in some countries.

"But this is America,"
Heather says.
"And burping's
not good
etiquette, except
maybe in Connecticut
but not in
Texas."

Bio-Dad lives in
Connecticut. I'm
glad that he lives
too far
to star
in the story
of my
life.
He has a new
wife,
and another
daughter,
and that's

where Walter the
Bio-Dad ought to
be: at home
with his
real-life family.

I've admitted my fib
about Blake
and the Great Date Rape.
Mom's going to take
a while to get over this,
I can tell.
I might as well
accept
that I'll be kept
on Mom's shit list
for at least
a decade or two.
Maybe by the time
I turn thirty,
she'll have stopped her
dirty looks
and nasty cuts.

Mom's been snapping
about crap that doesn't matter.
"Pick up that backpack!" she snaps.
"Stop snacking!

Stop cracking that gum!
Stop hacking when you cough!
Wipe off that mascara, Sahara!"
Next thing you know,
she'll be yelling at me
for breathing and my heart beating.
The noise will annoy her.
My life will destroy her.
Everything bad in this damn world
is Sahara's fault.
Blame it all on Walt.
He helped to make me.
She's pissed that I even exist.
Mom could have been the
Queen of Everything
without me.
I've ruined her freaking life.

Mom's still ragging
me, nagging me
about how I
should or could
call Dustin.
"It would
be a good
move. What
if he hears
it through
the grapevine?"

"He won't,"
I say.
"It's cool for me
that he's
not in the
same school."

"But he has
to know," Mom
insists. She's
pissed.

"Why?" I ask.

"Because
he's the
father,"
Mom says.

"He's Bio-Dad.
That's it.
That doesn't
mean shit.
This kid
will be fine
without
him."

My eyes
brim.
The kid
that swims
inside of me
will someday
lie to me,
and I'll lie
to it
by telling
the kid
that its
Bio-Dad
is dead.

I'm dreaming
that someone
is screaming.
I wake up.
My stomach rolls.
Somebody really is screaming,
in the living room.
No; it's not screaming.
It's weeping.
It's creepy.
It's giving me
the heebie-jeebies.
I sneak

into the living room,
and the TV
is on.
It's a religious show,
with some preacher
who thinks he knows
everything when
normal people are sleeping.
Mom's holding the phone.

Ohmigod.

She's talking about me
and my pregnancy
to some person I can't even see.
She's weeping
in between the sentences
about her pregnant teen.
"Please pray for me," she blubbers.
I hover.
She is *so* busted.
I'm way disgusted.

Mom's eyes
are puffed.
I've seen enough.
I've heard enough.
If Mom thinks that *she*
has it rough, I'd like to see

her walk in my shoes
for a week,
with swollen feet
and ankles the size of thighs.
I'm the one
who should weep.
I try to go back to sleep,
but I keep
thinking about how people
on TV
know all about me.
Maybe Mom should call
the Oprah Show.
Then the whole world would know.

Cadbury eggs
are my best
friends, and
my Easter eating
of them
never ends.
I've had ten
dozen
at least.
I'm a beast.
I have ham,
biscuits with jam,
and cheese on Spam.

I have yellow marshmallow
Peeps, green jelly
beans, and hollow
chocolate bunnies.

Heather thinks it's
funny that her
little sister
is so big.
I'm a freakin'
pig.
This pregnancy gig
is no picnic.
The baby kicks.
It rolls and flips.
My hips
are ships.
I can't zip
my Fashion Bug
way-too-snug
maternity jeans.
I can't sleep.
I can't stop eating.
My belly button
shows through
my clothes,
and even my
freakin' nose
is swollen.

My tops are tight.
This bites.
The buttons strain.
What a pain.
My boobs are huge.
My butt has grown,
and I loaned
all my old clothes
to Heather,
who's light as
a feather.

"Your butt
is doubled,"
she says.
"It's a bubble."

"Don't go to the trouble
of studying
my butt," I snap.
"That's crap.
Just take
my self-esteem
and mush
it into Cadbury cream."

Somebody put
wipes and diapers—

Huggies and Pampers—
in my Easter basket.
They might as well
build a casket
for the old Sahara.
She's gone forever.

Heather sucks.
So does Curt.
I won't give my kid
a sibling
because brothers
and sisters
are a waste
of space.
And the
freaking
Easter Bunny
is so
not funny.

Mom's giving me
the Silent Treatment.
This could last
for weeks.

She's on a spree
of shopping

and going for massages
and manicures
and pedicures
and facials.
I think that she's going crazy.
I think that she's afraid
to face reality.
I think that she's evading
the eventuality of my baby.
The lady is using a tanning bed,
for God's sake!
She looks fake.

Her hands are perfect.
Her feet are perfect.
Her hair is perfect.
Her skin is tanned.
She's working out.
She's had her teeth whitened
and her hair lightened.
This is really kind of frightening.
I think that Mom's having
a midlife crisis.

She's no longer the Mom
I've always known.
Mom's dressing hip.
She's flipped.
She's a freaking Barbie doll

who will soon be a grandma.
Maybe she's pampering herself
before she needs to help Pamper
a baby.
Maybe she's in denial
about her old age.
Mom needs to wake up
and smell the coffee
and stop looking like a blonde
Mafia mom.
Just because she *looks* perfect
doesn't mean that everything will be
okay.
Life isn't that way.
Maybe I'll go blonde some day.

I'm calling Dustin.

"Don't go bustin'
on him," Curt says.
 "Break it gentle."

"Don't be mental," I say.
"This is all
his fault."

Curt salts his fries
and rolls his eyes.

"Fine. It's also mine," I say.
"It's my fault, too.
I had no freakin' clue.
What do you think
he'll do?"

Curt shrugs.
This bugs me.
"What would
you do?" I ask Curt.
"What if you
were a father?
Would you bother
with the kid?"
"I'm not an idiot!" Curt says.
"Of course, I'd bother!
I'd be a rockin' father!"

"Yeah, right.
And P. Diddy is white."

"Dustin will do right
by you. You just have
to tell him what you want him
to do."

I don't know what I want him to do.
Disappear and go live somewhere
far from here? Pay child support?

Go to court
and win parental visitation?
Marry me and turn me
into a mental patient?

I'm dialing the number.
This is such a bummer.
I wish that it was summer,
and this was all a bad memory.

This too shall pass.
Dustin won't always be
a pain in my ass.
Someday I'll laugh
about these things.

The phone rings.
I get the answering machine.
"Leave a message," it says.
It beeps.
I take a deep
breath.
"Dustin, it's Sahara.
Call me as soon as possible.
I'll be going
to the hospital."

There's a click.
The baby kicks.

"What's up?" Dustin says.
I take a breath.
My heart feels like death.

"I'm pregnant," I blurt.
Curt shakes his head.

"By who?" Dustin asks.

"By you," I reply.

"It's not mine," Dustin says.

"Fine," I reply.
"It's mine.
It's all mine,
And I'll …
we will be just fine."

"Good-bye," he says.

I wish that he
was dead.
I regret the day we met.
No. I don't.
His loss.
My gain.
My baby.
My pain.

They know now.
The whole school knows.
I can no longer
see my toes.
My belly button pokes
through my clothes.
People look Somewhere Else
when I waddle
into the room.
They gossip
about who might be
the father.
I don't even bother
to defend myself.

My stomach is a shelf.
The cafeteria gets still
while I fill my tray
and balance it on my stomach.
I use a wheeled backpack now.
It's so lame.
Nobody asks if I'm going
to the game.
Nothing is the same.
I wish that I lived
in the 1950s,
when girls like me
were sent away

in secret, in privacy,
to Homes for Unwed Mothers.

I think it'd be better
to be in a place
where *everybody*
is a disgrace.

Holy shit.
The contractions
have hit.
My body
is at war
with me.
I'm at war
with my body.

Holy shit.
Owww. Pow.
Every five
minutes,
it's hitting.
A belt
of steel,
trying to
squeeze
the life
out of me.

Breathe.
Don't die.
Don't cry.
It'll be fine.
It won't kill you.
It'll come out.
OWWWWW.

Pain attacks.
It radiates:
front,
back.
This is it.
Holy shit.
I'm in labor.
I'm going to
be a mom.
A bomb
explodes,
and water
gushes,
quick liquid.

Holy shit.
This is it.
I'm having a kid.

"MOM-MY!
HELP ME!"

She comes running,
my mama.
My Sponge Bob pajamas
are soaked.
This is no
joke.
It's not a dream
or a show on TV.
I'm having
a kid.
Holy shit.
"Breathe, Sahara.
Stay calm.
Let's go."

How can I go
when I don't know
how to walk?
I can't even talk.
There's a hulk
inside of me,
trying to get
out of me.

"OWWWWW!"

Somehow
Mom gets me
to the door.

The war
is getting worse.
"Fuck. This …
sucks. Ouch.
Can I just lay
on the couch?"

"Don't curse," Mom says.

"It's getting worse.
I need a hearse.
It's killing me."
I'm doubled
over my bubble
of hurt.
Curt stares.
I don't care.
All of a sudden
I wonder
about my hair.
This is unbearable.
I bet I look
terrible.
I'm at war.
I'm an army of one—
no, two.

We go
out the door.
I hate this war.

Mom's driving
fast.
It's a full
moon.
We pass
the school.
Cool. No school
for me
today: May 8.
This is way
surreal.
I don't know
if I can deal.

"OWWWW!"

"Where's your
suitcase? Didn't
you pack a bag?
I told you to pack
a bag."

Leave it to my mom
to nag
at a time
like this.
I'm pissed.
Mom just

missed hitting
a tree.
I think
she's trying
to kill me,
and the
baby.

Is this a dream?
I scream.
A cat dashes
in the beam
of the headlights.
My stomach is tight.
It squeezes. *Jesus.*
"Think about this," Mom says,
"before the next time you think
about having unprotected sex."

I'm never having sex again.
I'll be a permanent virgin.

We're at
the hospital.

Wet.

*Get her into
delivery.*

Pain.
It's a race
except I'm
not running.
I'm in a
wheelchair,
pushed by
a nurse.
Everything's
a blur,
and my insides
have burst.

Flat.
My back.
My gut.
Knees up.
Stirrups.
Cold.
Steel.
Voices.
No more choices.
Inside of me.
Outside of me.
Breathe.
In.
Out.
In.
Out.

In.
Out.
Out.
In.
A doctor.
Mom.
Nurse.
Silver.
White.
Light.
Bright.
It's going to kill me.
Push.
PUSH … PUSH …
Mom's face is red.
She's breathing heavy, too.
She yells,
"I see the head!"

Am I dead?

The pain
is insane.
Baby.
Me.
Me.
Baby.
Into the world.

It's a girl.

I'm holding it.
Holy shit.
I had a baby.
I *have* a baby.
It's red.
It's not dead.

I'm laughing
and crying
at the same
time.

"Ohmigod. Ohmigod.
Is she okay?"

"She's beautiful,"
says a nurse.
"Perfect. Ten fingers.
Ten toes. Your nose."

I kiss the baby's head.
"Welcome to the world,
little girl," says the doctor.

She's mine,
and she's fine.

Nine months ago,
she was a pink line.
I start to cry.
So does she.

I'm a mother,
and we're now
each other's
family.

She's straight
from another
place, and I'm
naming her … Grace.

I'm in
total love.
I love her
wiggly fingers.
I love her
teeny toes.
I love her
tiny nose.
I love her
eyes
and her cries
and her
thighs.

I love her
head
and her
lips
and her
face.
I don't
have space
inside of me
for so
much love.
It overflows.
I float.
I gloat.
My heart is butter.
Her belly button
will be a souvenir
of the nine months
that we were attached
by a magical cord.
She's part of me,
and I'm part of her,
for eternity.

I hope
that she
loves me
as much
as I love her.

She's the world.
The world is her.

She's eight pounds,
one ounce,
and I want to announce
it to the universe.

I'm going to nurse!

I can't stop staring
at her: the baby Grace.
She has a face.
She looks like me.
She came out of me.

She is me
and I am her,
and me and
the earth
will never be
the same,
now that
we have
Grace.

Emma's in school,
on another planet.

I know
that she has
her phone,
even though
cell phones
are not allowed
to be used
in school.

I text-message her:
IAG.
It's a girl.
And then,
I return to
my world,
my new universe:
nursing
my baby,
my Grace.

We're going
home.
A nurse
pushes
us in a
wheelchair
through
the halls,

along the walls
of the
hospital.

I'm
holding
my baby
next to
my heart.
Her sleeper
is pink,
and so is
her hat.
I'm still fat,
but it doesn't
matter.
I'm going
to protect
my baby
and keep her safe
because
the world
is a dangerous
place.
There are
fires and floods
and blood
and cuts
and bureaus

that fall
on babies.
There are
cords that strangle
and things
that mangle,
but I'll keep
this baby safe
because life,
death, and
everything
in-between
depends
on me.

I'll do my best
and leave the rest
to fate.

Someday Grace
will have a date,
and I'll wait,
and yell at her
if she's late.

I'm now a mom,
and maybe my baby
will grow up to
go to the prom.

Maybe I'll allow
Bio-Dad to visit.
Maybe I'll give Dustin
another chance.
Maybe I'll ask Aunt Heather
and Emma
to baby-sit
every now and then.
I need to go to the gym.
I need to get a crib.

But for now
I just want to go
to the Old Navy
for babies
and get Grace
something made
of fleece.

"Listen," I whisper.
"I'll have you
christened. Catholics
can be funny about stuff
like this,
but I'll take
care of it.
I promise.
I'll take care
of everything.

You can count
on me, and don't
you *ever* have an
unwed pregnancy."

The nurse pushes
us through the door
and into the world.
I'm nervous.
How on earth
will I do this?
Yesterday is dead.
Forever is ahead.
I'm a new person,
and I've made a new human.
The sun is shining.
The baby burps.
My stitches hurt.

Mom waits at the curb.